GIGI

A Story of Forbidden Love and Consequence

BY DANIEL T. WILLIS, SR.

DORRANCE
PUBLISHING CO
EST. 1920
PITTSBURGH, PENNSYLVANIA 15238

Dorrance Publishing Co
585 Alpha Drive
Suite 103
Pittsburgh, PA 15238
Visit our website at *www.dorrancebookstore.com*

ISBN: 979-8-8902-7171-6
eISBN: 979-8-8902-7669-8

GIGI

A Story of Forbidden Love and Consequence

CHAPTER ONE

Angeline Valmond-Schmidt stared menacingly at the rotating ceiling fan. An antique grandfather clock in the living room chimed twelve times. *Where the hell is he?* She sat upright on the pastel king comforter, whisked strands of wavy black hair behind each ear, moved to the side of the bed and slammed both feet on the floor.

"Hunt's Distributors, how may I direct your call?"

"Warehousing, please."

"One moment."

"Warehousing, Jonathan speaking?"

"Yes. May I speak to Albert Schmidt?"

"Whom shall I say is calling?"

"His wife…Angeline."

A momentary silence.

"Er, ma'am, Albert's not here. In fact, he clocked out hours ago. Have you tried his cell phone? He may be stuck in traffic…."

"No, but I will. Thank you."

Two beeps squelched that need.

"Albert?"

"Hey, baby. Looks like I'm gonna have to pull a double shift. One of the guys called in sick…."

Angeline felt the blood rush to her head. "No, I understand. I'll see you in the morning, then."

"See you then. Love you…."

"Love you, too."

The phone sailed across the room like an errant frisbee.

"You son of a bitch!!!"

A startled teenage boy jumped from his twin bed and ran down the hall. He knocked twice on the door.

"Mom? You okay? Mom?"

No answer. He turned the knob.

Angeline sat rigid, shaking, oblivious to his presence. Tears ran down both cheeks.

Jean Claude fell to his knees at his mother's feet. Her eyes dropped slowly, acknowledging him for the first time. But she did not see her son—she saw just another pitiful member of the male species.

"Get away from me!" she exclaimed, shoving him with both hands.

He quickly sprang back up, gripping both her legs. "Mom! What's wrong? Please let me help you…."

Tears began to trickle down the face of the young man she finally recognized. She wiped them away and held his cheeks.

"Jean Claude? Oh, my darling!" She held him close and began to sob openly. "I'm so sorry, dear. Mommy's having a rough night, that's all…."

The concerned tenth-grader rested his chin on her right shoulder. He glanced across the room behind her at the master bathroom. The door was open. It was dark. Time passed slowly as he resolved to hold her—at least until she stopped shaking.

"Where's Dad? Shouldn't he be here by now? Shall I call Doctor Kisner?"

Angeline was prone to migraine headaches.

"He's working late tonight, precious. And no…I'm fine now. Just need to lie down."

She released him and stood to pull back the comforter. Jean Claude moved to give her space.

"You sure, Mom? I can stay until you fall asleep…."

"No, dear. Go back to bed. You've got a long day ahead. Classes and practice…I'll be fine."

Reluctantly, he walked backward to the door. Angeline climbed into bed, pulled the covers to her neck and smiled as he left the room.

CHAPTER TWO

Broadway 17th was every bit as hectic as Manhattan Boulevard back home. The black Mercedes AMG GT took the McIver exit. After three stoplights in short succession, Jean Claude decided to find someplace to wait it out. He turned right onto a dirt road and drove for several minutes. About a half-mile ahead to the left, a quaint chalet sat on a lot that seemed perfect. He pulled around back and parked the car.

Paduah was an Indonesian immigrant, an avid homeopath. She worked in an alternative medicine shop owned by her father, Ibrahim "Doc" Tarak. While browsing the aisles, Jean Claude stopped at a display of talismans shaped like monkeys, snakes, and mice. The sign above read *Assorted Gregory*.

"May we help you?" The soft, sweet voice was a perfect complement to the background music in the air.

Jean Claude turned to marvel at the vision of loveliness: hazel eyes, arched brows, mahogany skin, mid-length black hair in an apple cut. A ruby pendant drew attention to her forehead.

As she stepped from behind the cash register, Paduah's tapered forest green service coat did little to conceal the buxom breasts underneath.

"I was wondering about the Assorted Gregory…."

"Gris-gris serves many purposes, sir. Heart, digestive health and, oh, yes…contraception."

He remembered Olivia's obsession with having a baby. Paduah smiled as if she could read his mind.

"How does it work?"

"You wear it on the body."

"I mean for contraception. Is it like a chastity belt?"

Her high-pitched laugh almost sounded like a shriek.

"No, sir. It comes with a string attachment. You tie it around the neck and lower the image to the chest. Its essence then enters the body—"

"Paduah! Do not strike fear in the heart of the customer with old wives' tales." Doc placed a gentle hand on her shoulder, then turned to Jean Claude. "There is an ointment that comes with it, sir. The salve does the work. The image has more of a spiritual connotation. You know, like a crucifix or rosary beads to one who is Catholic."

Jean Claude chose one of the mice packages and headed for the register. He figured it would add some spice to he and Olivia's foreplay sessions, while keeping her ultimate goal in check. Doc returned to the storeroom for inventory.

Standing at the counter, Jean Claude reached for his American Express card, all the while staring at Paduah's chest. He looked up and handed it to her, half expecting a look of subtle disapproval. Instead, she smiled broadly and stroked his fingers as she took it.

"May I see your driver's license, please?"

They chatted briefly after the sale before he left the store.

Subsequent visits led to longer conversations, coffee, dinner and a movie, and eventually a romantic weekend in Aspen.

Paduah was extremely passionate—virtually insatiable. Her father was very protective and kept most potential suitors at bay. More than once he'd threatened Jean Claude with severe repercussions should his daughter be hurt in any way.

Unfortunately, the sun had set on their six-month relationship. Paduah was beginning to want more than he was willing to offer her—or any other woman, for that matter, right now….

Chapter Three

The hand-painted, heart-shaped sign at the rear entrance matched the one in front—*Paradise Massage*. Jean Claude got out of the car and went inside. The dimly lit hallway made the journey intriguing. A young blonde slid the double-paned glass window open and smiled.

"Hi there. What can we do for you today?"

Jean Claude read the large poster on the wall behind her.

"Think I'll have the one-hour Shiatsu."

"Great choice! Why don't you have a seat and someone will be out shortly."

She pointed to a set of six folding chairs separated by a magazine rack nearby. He sat down and picked up a copy of *Field & Stream*. Midway through the *Hunting and Fishing* section, a door opened.

"Sir, we're ready for you now."

The tall brunette wore a white smock with a stethoscope. Jean Claude followed her shapely hips to a small cubicle, where she scanned his temperature and took his blood pressure.

"120 over 75," she said. "Would you like to take a shower?"

"Yes, please. Been sitting at my desk all day and stuck in traffic for the past hour. Could use some freshening up."

She led him to the spa room down the hall.

"Soap and shampoo are beside the stream attachment. Towels directly outside the shower to your left. You can wrap one of the large ones around you afterward. Bring your clothes with you. It'll be the first door to the right on the way back. A masseuse will join you there. Enjoy."

Twenty minutes later, Jean Claude sat inside the pink rectangular room on an upholstered burgundy massage table. *Kenny G's* "Songbird" created a soothing atmosphere. He'd arranged his clothing neatly on a black leather chair next to an oak wood desk with an oil finish.

An Asian angel entered, also wearing a white smock, and closed the door behind her. Tall, long, brown hair with blonde highlights, bright red lipstick. She observed his chest, legs and feet before speaking.

"You police?"

"Nope, stockbroker…."

Angel removed her smock, placing it on the wrought-iron door hanger. She stood like a model at the end of a runway, wearing a baby-blue Victoria's Secret bra-and-panty set with a matching negligee drapeover.

She walked over to the desk, opened the top drawer and opened a dark brown pouch. She then reached for a zig-zag and a ceramic ashtray. After sprinkling the leafy green contents, she rolled it carefully into form, licked the seal and placed it in her mouth. After moistening it, she pulled with a twisting motion. She reached into a cannister on the desktop to retrieve a BIC lighter.

Angel took a long draw and handed the blunt to a delighted Jean Claude. He took two hits and gave it back. An instant feeling of euphoria came over him. She took one more hit, moistened her fingers, put it out and placed the unused portion in the ashtray.

"We begin now. You lay down, okay? On stomach."

The Asian angel began massaging one leg at a time. Starting with the feet, she skillfully manipulated his toes, soles, ankles and insteps, pausing periodically for more jasmine oil. She then kneaded his calves and hamstrings, stopping short of the glutes.

"Very nice…you exercise much, yes?"

"Not as often as I should. Played football, though, from middle school through college."

"Oh, I see… Good for you, I think. Look like Greek statue!"

"Thank you."

She worked with both hands, moving from bottom to top, top to bottom, with straight and circular motions, briefly brushing his anus along the way. Jean Claude felt his muscles tighten.

"Oh, sorry…I hurt you?" she said, pausing.

"No. No, it feels great, actually…," he said, dreading the moment he would be asked to turn over.

Angel adjusted the towel for access to his lower back. From there, she moved to the lats, triceps, shoulders and nape of the neck. She leaned over to whisper in his ear.

"Okay. You turn over now…."

Jean Claude held the towel in place while changing positions. She spent some time around the kneecaps before focusing on his quads. She worked the thighs with vigor, pausing when she saw the huge bulge at the towel's center. She looked up at Jean Claude's now flushed face, down at the bulge, back at him, then back to the bulge. She gently pried his fingers loose and removed the towel.

An invigorated penis jumped to attention. Her eyes widened. She leaned back and looked again at Jean Claude.

"I massage this too?"

He nodded.

"That cost more…."

"How much?"

"Eighty."

"Okay. My wallet is in my pants on the chair."

She found it, he paid her, she left the room. When she returned, Jean Claude lay waiting. She picked up a bottle of Jurgens lotion behind the jasmine oil and sat beside him. After pumping the nozzle four times, Angel rubbed her hands together.

Jean Claude closed his eyes. The lingering high sent him back in time—to one unforgettable night....

Chapter Four

The squeaking African Cherry wood door announced the arrival of an unexpected visitor. A quick shuffling of bedding followed a flick of the nightlight. The boy turned over on his side and closed his eyes.

"Jean Claude?"

Angeline stood at bedside wearing a velvet robe. Jean Claude feigned grogginess, reached for the light switch, rolled over and squinted.

"Mom? What's wrong? Dad late again?"

She sat next to him. The mattress dipped at his waist.

"It's after midnight. I noticed the light under your door. Why are you still awake?"

"Just cramming, Mom. I'm a little worried about this next exam…."

Angeline noticed the overturned magazine and box of Kleenex beside him. She reached across his lap and flipped it over—*Gallery's Girl Next Door: Meet Shelly Sumpter*. Jean Claude sat upright with his back against the headboard. His knuckles sank into the mattress on both sides.

"Well, what do we have here? Might this exam, by any chance, be in your Human Anatomy class?"

Jean Claude froze in a state of busted silence. Angeline turned the pages to the centerfold. Shelly stood bare-chested, holding the reins of a thoroughbred in a beautiful pasture.

The disheveled robe drifted open, flashing full breasts and a barely discernable pair of red-laced panties. Jean Claude could not believe his eyes! Two mounds rounded to perfection, long, jutting nipples, tight stomach…. His mom was a centerfold! He fought to restrain a most unwelcome involuntary lower-body reflex.

Angeline felt the intermittent poking at her ribs. She sat up and the bulge was on full display. Jean Claude's hands left his sides to cover his face. He resisted, but she shook her head and lowered them.

"This is nothing to be ashamed of, dear…."

She slowly pulled the covers down to his knees. He wasn't wearing briefs. A full-blown erection basked in the nightlight.

"Damnit, Mom!"

His entire body blushed.

"It's me, Jean Claude. I changed your diapers. Bathed you. Taught you hygiene. I know your body as well as you do. Now relax and talk to me…. Do you have a girlfriend?"

Jean Claude blinked twice. "What? No, Mom. With classes and practice…I haven't had the time or energy—"

His mother was no longer listening.

"Mom! What are you doing? You can't—"

Angeline raised a finger to his lips.

"Sssh…. You're getting to an age where you need more than a magazine and tissue. You need companionship…someone you can share these things with…."

Jean Claude tried to protest, but her experienced fingers tempered the urge. She paused to shed the robe and placed his member between her breasts, giving him stroke after stroke of pleasure he'd never felt before. Soon a familiar rush of pressure rumbled up the shaft. His penis hardened in preparation. He screamed as she took him past her lips, over her tongue and down her throat….

Another powerful release interrupted the drug-induced flashback. The angel was long-pumping him with slow, finishing strokes. His eruption covered her fingers, the back of her hand, and left jagged lines along her rosy cheeks. She stood and headed for the stainless-steel basin in the far corner, returning minutes later with a warm towel.

"What's funny?"

Angel had giggled after wiping his testicles clean.

"You make much noise. Then call me Mom. Customer never did that before…."

"Sorry…I didn't realize—"

"No problem. Made me laugh."

Jean Claude swung his legs around the side. The soft leather made a Whoopi Cushion sound. He and Angel laughed while he dressed.

"That was great. I'll be back for sure."

Angel grabbed the smock and handed him a card: *Jennie Po— Massage Therapist, LMT.* It went in his lapel pocket. She touched his arm at the door.

"You come back…ask for me, okay?"

"Sure thing, Jennie. Until then…."

CHAPTER FIVE

It was a cold autumn morning. The deoxidized copper radiator in the hallway offered little relief from outside draft. Jean Claude stepped out of his bedroom ready for school.

Angeline stood at the center island of her concave kitchen cutting bell peppers, onions and tomatoes. She wore last night's robe, now with flannel pajamas underneath. A Pyrex bowl of scrambled egg yolks sat on the counter alongside measured portions of sea salt, black pepper and sage.

The still-disoriented sophomore admired the way her nimble fingers manipulated the vegetables. He thought about last night.... She didn't seem to notice him taking a seat at the breakfast table.

"Good morning, dear," she said without looking up. "Bet you're good and hungry. Go ahead and get yourself a plate. This won't take long...."

She turned to the skillet on the stove with the bowl of eggs. Jean Claude got up, pulled a plate from the cabinet and stood next to her. The toes in his Adidas curled.

"Mom? About last night...."

Angeline used a wooden spatula to spread the eggs in the pan. She reached for the vegetables.

"What was that all about? I don't under—"

"*Endoctrinement* is what we call it back home, honey. Here, the word, I believe, is indoctrination."

She flipped the omelet and slid it onto his plate. She then gathered toast, orange juice and a glass as he took a knife and fork from the drawer.

"In my day," she said, filling his glass, "parents took the time to fully prepare children for life after they leave home. Fathers taught the boys to work and provide for their families. Women taught their daughters to nurture their children and the importance of loyalty to their husbands."

Jean Claude chewed slowly, waiting for the full explanation.

"Sex education was not taught in schools back then. Parents were expected to fulfill that necessity. Men introduced their girls to sex, while women instructed the boys."

"But I thought girls were raised to be virgins when they got married back then…."

Angeline laughed and touched his shoulder. "A myth, baby… based on American folklore steeped in inhibition. Truth is, men prefer virgins for marriage but have affairs with experienced women who will give them what they don't get from their naïve wives at home."

"Does Dad know how you were raised?"

"Heavens no, dear! I kept that part of my past from him for fear he'd think less of me. On our wedding night, I screamed like a banshee. When it was over and he got up to go to the bathroom, I used a bottle of ketchup I kept in my purse by the bed to simulate the expected. Sweet innocence is what he wanted, so I gave him that. A mistake I now deeply regret…."

Jingling keys at the front door confirmed Albert's arrival. He walked in briskly rubbing both arms. He was tall, blond hair, broad shoulders and bushy eyebrows. He looked fresh, especially for someone who'd just worked a double shift. His hair was neatly combed, face and hands free from occupational grime. He looked at Angeline, then at Jean Claude.

"Burr! Must be sub-forty degrees out there.... Hey, Tiger! Ready to hit that academic grind again today?"

He smiled and closed the door.

"Yes, sir."

"Good! You'll need a scholarship to get into Syracuse, you know."

"I know, Dad."

Albert walked to Angeline and bent over. She offered him a half-hearted tilt for a peck on the cheek.

"Hi, baby girl. Smells great in here. Got some o' that left over for me? I'm starving!"

"Sure. Be just a few minutes...."

She rolled her eyes and moved toward the refrigerator.

"Sounds great!" He began unbuttoning his burlap trench coat.

"Jean Claude...," Angeline spoke as-a-matter-of-fact, "find a woman who'll prioritize your physical and mental wellbeing. One with a conservative mind, but not hampered by inhibitions. Someone willing to give her absolute all. And if you cannot do the same for her, if you can't give her the man she wants...the man she needs...let her go! Don't waste her time. Don't be a son of a bitch!"

Jean Claude watched the smile disappear from his father's face. Albert looked at Angeline, then moved quickly to the master bedroom. Jean Claude brought his empty plate to the sink. He looked at his mom with eyes that understood for the first time as he whispered in her ear.

"So last night was about me...not exactly sure what *I'm* supposed to do...."

While reaching for more eggs, she whispered back, "Be patient, dear. You've only had one session...."

One session became two, then three, evolving from curriculum to covenant between teacher and student, mother and child. Shrouded in secrecy, tainted with incest, justified by tradition. Given room to flourish by the neglect of a philandering husband. Jean Claude's *Endoctrinement* would last until he left for college....

CHAPTER SIX

"Ocean Prime – Larimer Square. Marjorie speaking, may I help you?"

"It's Jean Claude Valmond, beautiful. I'd like to make a reservation for tonight. Think you can do that for me?"

"Anything for you, Mr. Valmond. How many colleagues will we be accommodating this time?"

"Not that kind of meal, sexy. Need a table for two. Preferably somewhere between seven and eight o'clock."

"How about seven-forty-five?"

"That'll work! See you then."

He hung up and made the next call.

"Hello?"

"It's all set, baby. Be there in an hour."

"Thank goodness! I've missed you so much…."

On the way, horns blew from a cavalcade of limousines, led by a red Mazda with a "Just Married" bumper sign. Paduah gasped, raising hands to mouth. Her eyes twinkled.

Now seated, the Maître d' handed each one a menu. Sometime later, a man arrived dressed in a red blazer, white shirt and slacks and a black bowtie. They were ready to order.

"Good evening. My name is James and I'll be serving you tonight. What would you like to order?" he said with pen and pad, looking first to Paduah.

"I'll have the sea scallops with parmesan risotto, English peas, and citrus vinaigrette." She slapped playfully at her left hand. "My father would die if he heard me utter those words."

Jean Claude smiled. "I'll have the ten-ounce filet mignon, with a baked potato, asparagus, and braised garlic bread. Oh, and bring us a carafe of your finest cabernet."

"Right away, sir, ma'am." He took both menus, nodded and disappeared.

"What is Doc's problem with sea scallops?"

"To him, if it's not curried, it's not food," she said.

Jean Claude smirked and folded his arms.

"Apparently, he has a problem with more than just your dietary choices."

"What do you mean?"

"Did you see the look on his face when I opened the car door for you?"

"Oh, that…don't mind him. Some things you just have to ignore."

"I don't know that I can anymore, Paddie…."

Paduah leaned closer.

"Jean…he's old-fashioned…Conservative…he's—"

"Your father!"

Paduah exhaled when the wine came.

"May I interest you in some dessert? The black forest cake is very popular tonight…," James said, standing behind the shiny aluminum display cart.

Jean Claude glanced at his Rolex. They hadn't spoken since the food arrived an hour ago. Paduah lifted the napkin from her lap, leaned forward and tapped her fingers on the white linen tablecloth.

"No, I don't think so, thank you. Check, please."

Jean Claude reached for his pen. Paduah smiled at James as the cart rolled away. She looked at Jean Claude with tight lips.

"What is wrong, Mr. Valmond?"

She raised her palms and shrugged her shoulders.

"Wrong?"

"Yes, wrong! You didn't dress me up and bring me to this lovely restaurant with great food to discuss my father's shortcomings.… What is really bothering you?"

Jean Claude scanned the lower level of the crowded room. A cheerful group of ice cream truckdrivers. A family of four dealing with a disgruntled toddler. Apparently, he didn't like the highchair the waitress provided. An Italian couple, holding hands and gazing into each other's eyes. A different world at every table.

He took both her hands. "Paddie…."

The passenger door flew open before the car stopped.

"Paduah! I'm sorry…Paddie…."

She scurried up the side steps in tears.

Jean Claude pulled away, convinced the job was done. He gave himself a mental pat on the back, knowing he would never have to call her again. No time to waste thinking about that, though—she'd be fine. A roundtrip ticket on the dining room table promised access to an event bustling with infinite possibilities.

Chapter Seven

The sun had set on another day in Kenner City. In the distance, fireworks painted the night sky with flashing hues of red, white, and blue. Georgina recognized the faint sounds of jubilation through her slightly open kitchen window. Shrove Tuesday!

She focused on two portraits—one at each end of the black granite center island—to pay respects: first to Queen Laveau, then Doctor John—the two founders of her faith. Rising from the ebony worship stool, the anxious apprentice took one last inventory of items along the countertop: six seance candles, four herb-filled mason jars, purpose dolls with matching pins and needles, assorted talismans of gris-gris and a chaff of snake essence.

After blowing out the candles, she headed for the shower, leaving the sanctuary for now. The time had come to prepare for tonight's events. The spirits had spoken: *"Your target awaits in New Orleans!"*

Jean Claude Francis Valmond was living life to the fullest. He'd parlayed a business degree into a successful career in Commodities, specializing in cattle, dairy products and corn for grain.

"Canneries will feed you, son, but heifers'll make you rich," Albert would always say. "And before you marry only to find yourself trapped in a world of perpetual boredom, get all the stray pussy you can!"

Mardi Gras was always a great way to advance that philosophy.

While strolling the raucous French Quarter streets, he noticed a woman maneuvering through the crowd. She was absolutely stunning: tall, well-proportioned body, long wavy black hair, ruby-red earrings, hazel eyes and smooth caramel skin. She was wearing a lowcut red sundress and a Louis Vuitton striped crossbody handbag with matching Espadrilles. He took another swig from the flask of Ojen.

When their eyes met, an awkward feeling of shock and awe overcame her. She knew somehow this was the man, but the spirits never spoke of his strong appeal, nor of how he would look in a white silk suit.

The two stopped short of each other's personal space at a colorful awning in front of the Ritz Café on Bourbon Street. For the first time in his life, Jean Claude felt insecure about meeting a woman. He stepped forward, extending his right hand.

"Hi. I'm Jean Claude—Jean Claude Valmond."

"Georgina—Georgina Poncetrain. My friends call me Gigi."

"Pleased to meet you, Gigi. Any friends or family here? You seemed to be looking for someone earlier."

"No, I prefer to do Strove Tuesday on my own. Apparently, you do too," she said, noticing the diamond stud in his right earlobe.

"Just me and my Henny," he said, patting the flask nestled in his droptop satchel.

Gigi smiled and moved closer. Her fingers slowly traced the snakeskin strap from his left shoulder, down his chest, settling on the Maverick & Co. bag at his right side.

"Any left?" she spoke in a deep, sultry voice.

"Absolutely!"

She closed her eyes and tilted her head back as he brought the container to her lips.

They spent the next several minutes getting to know each other. Jean Claude told her he worked for Direxion Capital in Denver. He was born in Manhattan. Gigi was a systems analyst for CenturyLink in New Orleans—born and raised in nearby Kenner City. His parents met at Ellis Island during the massive influx of immigrants in the early 50s. His father a goatherder from Berlin, his mother a dancer from Paris. Dreams of playing professional football ended with a series of injuries suffered in his senior year. He moved to Colorado shortly after college graduation.

Gigi's father, a welder by trade, was born in Heerlen, Holland. He came to America through Ellis Island around the same time as Jean Claude's parents. Her mother was a housekeeper for a wealthy Louisiana family, who hired her from former Texas sharecroppers in the 1960s. While on a grocery shopping errand, she walked past a construction site on LaFontaine Boulevard. A man fell two stories from a section of scaffolding. She ran to his aid and cradled his bleeding head until medical help arrived. They both swore it was love at first sight.

"Sounds like a fairytale come true…. Where are they now?"

"I lost them both in a house fire years ago."

Her eyes watered as she briefly looked away. Jean Claude touched her left shoulder.

"Hey, we're running out of the good stuff…refill?"

"Sure."

She wiped a lingering tear from the corner of her right eye and smiled.

Hours later they were having the time of their lives. They laughed, sang, and danced the night away. Halfway through the third flask, a loud gong rang from the public address system. As the closing song began to play from speakers along the rooftops, couples turned to each other for the customary last dance. Jean Claude looked up, recognizing the opening drumbeat and organ solo. He turned to Gigi and cleared his throat.

"I'm gonna take a little time. A little time to think things over...."

"Foreigner!" Gigi raised both hands to flushed cheeks.

"May I have this dance?"

He reached for her hands.

Time stood still as they melted into each other's arms. Gigi sank deeper into his embrace. Jean Claude wrapped his strong arms tightly around her lower back. His long fingers pulled her body even closer. Gigi slid both hands upward until her arms met behind his neck. The tall streetlamp illuminated their swaying bodies, making all others appear to be mere bystanders in the night.

"Can't imagine ever letting you go. I don't want it to end like this. Besides, I don't think I can make it back to the hotel without a great deal of embarrassment."

Gigi noticed the ever-growing presence poking her navel. "Looks like somebody else is feeling the same way," she said, glancing downward.

They lunged forward, engaging in a deep, long, primal kiss. Eventually, Gigi pulled back, gasping for air.

"I've got a better idea," she whispered.

Taking him by the hand, they ran like mischievous children toward an idol taxi parked two blocks away. Falling into the backseat, she addressed the startled driver.

"732 Village Road, Kenner City, please."

"Where we going?" Jean Claude said as the cab skillfully weaved its way through pedestrian traffic.

"My place, silly."

She slid close enough to caress his left thigh.

Chapter Eight

Paduah watched dust particles go right to left—past to present—board by board over the storeroom floor: coming to America at five, losing her virginity in the back seat of a Ford Focus at fifteen, a phase of promiscuity from sophomore to senior year at UCLA. Returning home to bury Jaya, her mother—a breast cancer victim—after graduation. The decision to put the future on hold, at least until Doc recovered. No sign of that five years later....

Approaching the west wall, a lifetime of debris was ready for disposal—closure. Prayers of Jean Claude being the one to do so were unanswered. It was over. She grabbed the dustpan, assembled the pile, and took care of it. The storeroom was immaculate.

On the north wall, a six-tier glass shelf housed a variety of crystal balls not used since Jaya was alive. Paduah chose the one labeled "Rose Quartz," seer of romance. She wiped it clean, set it on the floor in the middle of the room and lowered herself into a half-lotus position. Thoughts of a babbling brook in a quiet forest cleared her mind.

"Please help me...I need clarity...."

A rolling mist filled the globe. A clear circle opened at its center, revealing the devastating truth....

She remembered the stanchion of synthetic nylon for product segregation. Bloodshot eyes scanned the room to the east wall.

Doc strolled down the stairs humming "Yo Te Amo Maria" by a band of his favorite landsmen, The Tieleman Brothers. It was Saturday morning—typically the busiest day of the week—and he was anxious to get started. Opening the door to the main store, he was surprised to find it dark and empty. He walked into the storeroom. Freshly inventoried merchandise had been neatly arranged and the room shined like new money.

"Paduah, I love what you've done to the place, but I fear the time has gotten away from you, dear. It's past nine o'clock...."

A lone crystal ball sat a few feet away.

"Uh-oh…looks like you may have forgotten something...."

Doc moved to place it back on the shelf but stopped mid-stride when he noticed two images inside. It was Jean Claude and a woman he did not recognize, locked in an act of rigorous sexual abandon. His fingers trembled. The glass shattered as it hit the floor.

"Blue-eyed devil!!! Paduah! Paduah!!!"

He ran to the closed office door.

The stench of body fluids immediately overwhelmed him. Her lifeless body hung from the far corner rafter. Doc used the chair underneath to untie the primitive noose and lowered this horrible nightmare to his bosom. He screamed until he could no more. Denver police found him hours later, rocking her back and forth, trying to close her bulging eyes.

Light years away, at the tip of Alpha Centauri, Queen Laveau and Dr. John agreed to meet and discuss the events developing below.

"Why Centaurus, Queen? It's loud and unsettling."

"Solar outbursts from Lady Proxima, John. We can speak freely here. Fatima despises the brightness.... Your call sounded urgent. Are you worried about our apprentice?"

"Did I not say this would happen, Lavie? Too soon for her, I said. She's too green, I warned. We must consider an alternative or suffer the wrath of Fatima!"

"Relax, John. She's enroute to the sanctuary now with the mark in tow. Everything seems to be progressing according to plan."

"According to plan??? Can you not see the spell this target has cast upon her? Her attraction, her longing for him?"

"I fear you underestimate the power of a woman's charm, John. It takes a unique brand of sex appeal to lure a mark of this caliber."

"You call it sex appeal. I call it imminent failure. I can smell the musk of lust in her loins from way up here! I never thought she was ready for an assignment of this magnitude."

"And she never will be if we don't give her the chance to grow. She's a good Janie…let's agree to withhold judgment until this whole thing unfolds."

"Well, if what we've seen thus far is any indication, this will not end well. Looks like the fruit does not fall far from the tree, if you ask me. It's in the genes, Queen."

"Don't let your fixation on one practitioner's failure cloud your assessment of another. Georgina has the right to individuality. Her decisions—not her bloodline—should define her worth."

"Alright, all right, Lavie. We'll wait…."

CHAPTER NINE

Soon the taxi arrived at the secluded residence sitting on a hill at the end of Village Road. When Gigi reached for her purse, Jean Claude touched her right hand.

"I've got this," he said as he opened his wallet, paid and tipped the driver.

"Thank you, sir. You two have a great evening."

The driver smiled as they exited, made a quick U-turn, and disappeared into the night.

Jean Claude noticed the glazed gypsum stone front, etched Chalise windows, and the black concave floodlight shining at a ninety-degree angle from the roof. It accented the marbled porch and columned entrance.

"Nice," he said as they scurried up the winding concrete path.

As Gigi leaned forward to access the alarm's keypad, Jean Claude wrapped his arms around her waist. The material of her dress crept softly between her cheeks. She typed faster than ever before.

"Welcome, Georgina."

The buzzer and lock recognized the voice prompt.

Caught up in a whirlwind of passion, two bodies attacked the clothing that denied them access to one another. Jean Claude's satchel, coat, tie and shirt fell in the foyer. Gigi's purse and sundress dropped two steps later on the living room floor. Jean Claude's eyes widened when he saw that she was not only naked underneath, but her shaven pubic area glistened in the dimly lit room.

Gigi dropped to her knees, unfastened his belt, unzipped his pants, and pulled them down around his ankles. When she came up, his engorged member struck her forehead and reverberated like a diving board. She stared in momentary silence. He looked down and smiled. She returned the smile, then took him into her mouth as far as she could manage.

"Oh…my…God," he gasped as she quickly found her rhythm. "The bedroom…where…?"

She extended her right arm backward without missing a stroke. Reaching for her deltoids and triceps, the former athlete lifted her body until both legs encircled his waist. Taking hold of her hamstrings, he lifted once more, turned both palms upward at chest level, and sat her on his shoulders. His vicelike grip secured her back, giving her confidence to lean for better access. His experienced tongue drew circles around her vulva, periodically darting in and out of her vagina. A throbbing clitoris slipped between his soft lips.

Shockwaves of pleasure ran through her body like a colony of red ants. With one hand she grabbed a tuft of his curly hair, while pushing off the wall with the other as they moved irradicably toward the bedroom.

"Yesss…to your left…now straight…oooh…."

Gigi led him from memory through the pitch-black room. His knees bumped the side of the bed, causing them to tumble onto the mattress.

Jean Claude positioned his knees. Gigi waited with fear and eager anticipation as she felt the tip at her wet orifice. He entered her slowly, but purposefully: the head…quarter mark…halfway…to the hilt! Their tongues met in violent desperation, carrying both into a world seldom seen by two. Plans of a tragic endeavor—so clearly delineated just hours before—reduced to ashes in the fire that raged between them.

The flamboyant self-proclaimed ladies' man woke up dazed and confused. Last night was more than just sex. It was pure, surreal even. Their bodies performed as one entity, each instinctively responding to the needs of the other. Changing positions, speeds, levels of intensity, until time after time the Earth shook violently beneath them. They fell asleep, still joined, gazing into each other's bewildered eyes.

Gigi giggled when he reached for her, as she slid across the large mahogany sleigh bed, pausing suggestively over his alabaster body on her way to the kitchen. He groaned as she left the room.

But reality struck as soon as she entered the hallway. Feelings of sheer bliss quickly turned to horror and dismay as she approached the sanctuary. It was time to atone for last night's indiscretion.

Sometime later, Jean Claude paused, naked as he walked the narrow passageway. Golden-eyed Lions, Imagined Landscapes and Graffiti Roses lined the sky blue walls. The faint scent of Coco Mademoiselle tickled his nose. An unfamiliar feeling struck the depths of his soul. One for years he'd thought highly improbable, despite his mother's assurances. It felt like gliding in a corridor of cloudless blue skies....

But the brief flight over utopia met turbulence at the kitchen door.

Chapter Ten

"**D**ear, now you know the penalty for disobedience."

"But Queen, you do not understand. It was never my intention—"

"*Silence, child! This man has destroyed the lives of many women. Fatima will not be denied recompense!*" Dr. John's eyes blazed deep red. "*And what image is this you bring before us? Be you apprentice or exhibitionist?*"

Gigi's eyes widened. She raised both arms to her chest and clenched her legs together.

"*Fear not, Georgina. There is still time to right this wrong. Listen to me carefully….*"

After Queen's lengthy instruction, a reluctant and tearful Gigi approached the bedroom. Adjacent to the tousled cradle of iniquity, she saw the open sliding glass door leading to the backyard. Jean Claude must have noticed the scenic view when the morning sun hit the glass. Leaving her weapons in the hallway, she entered the room.

She moved toward the back door, stopping at the closet to retrieve a terrycloth robe. As she took it off the hanger, the full-length mirror captured her nakedness. Individual patches of skin discoloration covered her neck, breasts, stomach, and lower abdomen. Suddenly, she donned the robe, tied the belt in front, and clutched the collar to her throat.

Standing in the doorway, Gigi noticed the rear gate had been left ajar. Jean Claude was gone. She had mixed emotions—sadness for his absence, but grateful he would be spared his intended fate.

She'd been instructed to coat her lips with a sheer layer of snake essence and embrace the target with a kiss. The essence would render him paralyzed within seconds. She would then be able to disarticulate his body. Although he would've been able to feel the surgical onslaught, he would be unable to do anything but suffer the full experience of his own savage death.

"Goodbye, my love," she whispered. The morning breeze teased her hair and caressed her face. "No one's past is without flaws. I will intercede on our behalf and appeal to the spirits for leniency. If I am unsuccessful, I will forever remember the night we spent together...."

The dejected apprentice closed the glass door, drew the curtains, stood in the dark, and summoned the courage to report back. She took two steps and saw Jean Claude's white silk boxer shorts sprawled on the wood laminate floor at the foot of the bed. She felt a tingling sensation, remembering exactly how they got there. Picking them up, she sat on the side of the bed. Bringing the briefs to her nostrils, she drew a selfish reminder of his scent.

Unexpectedly, thoughts of her mother, Rafi, entered her mind. When Gigi was a teenager, Rafi, a seasoned practitioner, introduced her to the fundamentals of voodoo as part of an orientation to the cultural values of Choctaw Nation. Gigi never forgot the look on her mother's face when she severely chastened her, saying, "Gi, a decision to practice the craft is one of obligation, not choice. Once you make that decision, there is no turning back!"

Words Gigi never fully understood—until now. She carefully folded the underwear and placed it in her right robe pocket....

"This man has destroyed the lives of many women. Fatima will not be denied recompense!"

Not since college had speed been so vital. With knees raised, each stride fully extended, Jean Claude ran as though his life depended on it. Still squeezing the phone in his left hand, he approached the taxi on Napoleon Road.

"Mr. Valmond?"

The broad back and shoulders were masculine, but the voice soft and feminine—a mixture of Dutch and Choctaw Indian. The cab wreaked of Coco Mademoiselle.

Jean Claude sniffed his collar, thumb, index and middle fingers. He slumped in the back seat.

"Sir?" a now deep, raspy voice persisted.

"Uh, yes, of course. I'm Valmond."

The driver smiled into the rearview mirror and hit the I-10 on-ramp. Moments later, they arrived at The Roosevelt-Waldorf Astoria in New Orleans.

CHAPTER ELEVEN

Gigi gathered her tools and began the journey back to the sanctuary. In the distance, she noticed her sundress and purse had been neatly draped over the beige sectional in the living room. The rubber plant was restored to an upright position in the foyer. Jean Claude's clothes were gone. She longed to have had the chance to kiss him goodbye. Her right hand gently squeezed the briefs pocket.

Jean Claude stood showered and refreshed at the front desk. He looked dashing in Ralph Lauren activewear and Ray-Bans. The concierge hurried to meet him. His black suit, shoes, tie and crisp white shirt spoke to the integrity of the establishment. Aligned perfectly on his upper-right chest, a gold-plated rectangular name badge read "Michael Wolter-Baton Rouge, LA." Jean Claude reached for his wallet.

"Good morning, Mr. Valmond! I trust you enjoyed your stay."

"I certainly did, Michael…always do."

"Well, we're always glad to have you…."

His voice faded as another took its place.

"How could you leave me?"

Gigi stood wearing two of the hotel's bath towels—one around her body, the other wrapped around her head. Jean Claude blinked and stumbled backward.

"Careful, sir…are you alright?"

Michael leaned over the counter but couldn't reach him. Jean Claude recovered.

"No, I'm fine. Didn't get much sleep last night, that's all."

Michael flashed a wry smile. "Of course you didn't, sir. And, as usual, I've taken the liberty of reserving a breakfast table for two. Will someone be joining you shortly?"

"Not this time, Michael. I'll need a taxi to the airport."

"Right away, Mr. Valmond. Have a great flight, and we'll see you next time."

He motioned to a man in uniform at the front entrance, who smiled and nodded. Jean Claude extended the handle of his carryon luggage and rolled it away.

Gigi tightened her robe and entered the sanctuary.

"Servant, have you come to gather storage containers for the remains?"

Gigi lowered her head.

"Forgive me, Queen. There has been a development. The target has escaped."

"What do you mean escaped?" said Dr. John. *"Will a man leave the bed of his lover without so much as a goodbye?"*

"Yes, sir. When I returned to my bedroom, he was no longer there. I searched everywhere but—"

"Enough! This does not surprise me. An act such as this confirms his complete lack of moral character. The Goddess judged well to declare him unfit to live."

"But sir, I love him."

"What do you know of love? You, like your mother, have simply crumbled under the curse of the flesh!"

"Forgive me, sir. Why do you speak of my mother?"

"Rafi, like you, defied the will of Fatima for the lust of a man. Worse still, she married him—that Dutch whoremonger you called 'Daddy'!"

"Sir, are you saying the death of both my parents was—"

"Punishment for disobedience! Yes, apprentice. And now you too must suffer like consequence!"

Gigi's eyebrows drew closer together. She turned to Queen Laveau. "Queen, can you not reason with the Goddess on my behalf? I am but a lowly apprentice, with no experience in matters of the heart."

Tears trickled down her cheeks.

"I am sorry, dear, but Fatima's will is sovereign. There are no exceptions in the universe of Dalhama."

"But my efforts have been above reproach, thus far. If you would only take the time…."

"There is no time!" Dr. John interjected.

"There is no time," Queen Laveau conceded.

"There is no time." "There is no time…."

The two voices faded in a cloud of smoke as they repeated the words of doom. They would never return.

Chapter Twelve

Gigi sat in a cesspool of inertia. She tried to open the briefs pocket but could not move. From the window, a cloud seeped under the pane, over the sill and down the wall. It parted at the crown molding to travel in opposite directions. Every inch of black paint was wiped away as the room turned bright red. A large circle appeared before her and an all-too-familiar face took shape.

"Mother?"

"*Yes, Gi. I've come to take you home.*"

Rafi stretched out her hand to caress Gigi's left cheek.

"Oh, Mother…what have I done? Why must it end this way?"

The desperate apprentice reached for Rafi's hand, but her fingers passed through it. Rafi withdrew her hand and placed a finger to Gigi's lips.

"*Hush…no more questions, dear. Just know that I love you. Now we must prepare for departure….*"

She moved the finger to the séance candles, igniting each one with a touch. Gigi's legs trembled. The balls of her feet performed involuntary drumrolls on the floor. Rafi beckoned the chaff of snake essence. As it opened, a yellow python emerged, encircling Gigi's ankles. In seconds, the movement ceased. Gigi watched her arms drop to her sides. Her back straightened; the robe opened. One candle went out.

Two mason jars floated across the room and emptied their contents over her neck, chest, and abdomen. When the petals and roots hit the floor, all skin discolorations had vanished. A second candle lost flame.

A talisman of monkey-shaped gris-gris followed, tying itself around her neck and settling between her breasts. On cue, the python uncoiled and slithered back to its chaff. Another candle burned out.

A patch of smoke surrounded one of the purpose dolls. The doll became an exact replica of Gigi. It bounced over to her and climbed the exposed flesh to the top of her head. Assigned pins and needles fell into formation, taking aim from the center island. Gigi opened her mouth to scream but could not. The daggers fired with precision, landing on her neck, both breasts, abdomen, and pelvis. The fourth candle extinguished.

The darts formed a visible pattern down Gigi's frontal plane. Following the path, the cursed twin removed each one in passing. Drops of blood trickled from the vacant holes, as well as the teeth marks in Gigi's bottom lip. She fought through tears and pain to glare at her mother.

With bent knees, the doll propelled itself back onto the counter. It carefully distributed the collection of pins and needles around its feet. In a puff of smoke, the doll returned to original form. The fifth candle went out.

Rafi pointed to the gas stove. Each burner rotated to the HIGH position. She tapped Gigi gently on the forehead, lowering her unconscious body to the floor on her back. She then clapped three times.

"Georgina, come forth!"

A now radiant Gigi rose and stepped away from her earthly body. Rafi took her by the hand into the circle. They embraced. A brisk wind blew out the sixth candle.

The orbiting cloud dislodged the body's talisman and removed all remnants of the craft from the sanctuary. The circle vanished. The cloud dissipated, sending a bolt of lightning to the stove before exiting in the same manner it arrived.

Chapter Thirteen

Jean Claude's flight was sobering. A loss of cabin pressure, flashing lights and an animated flight crew made him realize just how temporal life really is. It felt good to be home. A red light on the marbled swan end table got his attention.

"You have fifteen messages."

"Hi, babe! It's me…Linda. Just calling to confirm our date for Saturday night. Can't wait to see you!"

Linda Fleischman. Her father, Edgar, made a fortune in dairy. Edgar introduced them during a company retreat at the Baymont a couple months ago. That night, she came to his hotel room. When Jean Claude opened the door, she raised a finger to her lips and walked in. Lovemaking was creative and energetic. If only he'd known she was just seventeen….

"Hey, lover." It was Mary Anne…Linda's mother. "I called to let you know Edgar will be out of town on business this weekend. I've got reservations at The Broadway Hilton for Friday night. So what do you say, around seven? Got something special for you…. Call me…."

He'd been meaning to evaluate that situation for its menage et trois potential. Right now, that endeavor seemed less appealing. He stopped playback and walked his luggage to the bedroom closet.

That night in a dream, he and Gigi were walking barefoot, hand in hand on a beach with white sand. They came to an alcove off the main body with a beautiful waterfall flowing from a rocky cliff. Gigi giggled—the way only she did—and dove in. He stripped down to t-shirt and briefs, jumped in, and they frolicked in the crystal-blue water.

Gigi went under and resurfaced moments later, handing him her dress, bra and panties.

"Take care of this for me…." Her whisper grazed his cheek.

He swam to shore, shed his underwear, placed the clothes on a nearby boulder and turned to look at her.

Suddenly, the water was gone and Gigi stood in a pool of murky clay. With her back turned to him, she sank slowly to her knees, then waist.

"Gigi!!!"

Jean Claude inched closer to the bank, frightened and desperate, his right arm extended.

She turned slowly to look at him, glanced at her waist, then back at him.

"Gigi, come toward me…move slowly…don't jerk…slow, smooth movements!"

Her stare was empty.

"I cannot, my love…I came to tell you it's going to be all right…. You did the right thing…. This is how it must be…. Remember me…. Goodbye, Jean Claude."

The clay rose to her chest and neck.

"No, Gigi!!! I won't leave you again!!! I need you!!! Come to me!!!"

He saw the tears as she smiled once more, kissed the air in his direction, and disappeared.

Jean Claude woke up in a cold sweat. The disheveled bedding left him uncovered and shivering. He rubbed his eyes and reached for the phone.

"American Airlines, how may I help you?"

Arriving at the Louis Armstrong Airport, he stopped briefly at the media center.

"What can I do for you, sir?"

"I'll have a double expresso with a honey twist."

As the stripe-shirted barista turned to the machine, Jean Claude made a mental note to load the 380 Mauser in his checked baggage. Whatever horror Gigi might be facing, she wouldn't be alone!

Several copies of the *Kenner Star* lay beside the cash register on the glass checkout counter. The conspicuous headline made him shudder:

"*Kenner Woman Found Dead After Fiery Home Explosion!*"

Jean Claude dropped to his knees, clutching the newspaper with both hands as he fought through tears to read confirmation of his worst nightmare.

"*Officials have identified the victim as West Lafayette Parish resident Georgina 'Gigi' Poncetrain….*"

The startled barista swung around suddenly, uncertain. Jean Claude rose and gently laid the *Star* on the glass.

"On second thought, this'll be all…."

He folded it and walked slowly back to the ticket counter. So many questions would never be answered. Most importantly, he could never hold Gigi in his arms again.

Chapter Fourteen

Back in Denver, Jean Claude picked up the phone to dial the first of many numbers from his rolodex. A frail voice answered.

"Hello?"

"Olivia…it's Jean Claude."

A long pause before the fragile voice became hostile—defiant.

"I have no desire to talk to you, Jean!"

"And you have every right to feel that way. But if you'll give me a minute of your time, I don't need you to talk…just listen. First of all, I owe you an apology…."

Olivia listened without interruption to Jean Claude's thirty-minute confessional. She then revealed a dark secret of her own. Termination of a six-week pregnancy. It was a boy. It was his. Complications from the abortion left her unable to have another child. A therapist helped her realize she was more obsessed with having a baby than being with Jean Claude. They eventually agreed to part ways amicably.

He methodically worked the list of nearly fifty women—an achievement he'd been so proud of just days ago—in an effort to right a world of wrongs. Some simply hung up the phone. Others fought to sustain the relationship. He was relieved to arrive at the last one.

"Yes?"

The man's voice was barely audible.

"Hello, Mr. Tarak. This is Jean Claude Valmond. Is Paduah available?"

Silence was followed by a soft groan.

"No, she is not."

"May I leave her a message?"

"That won't be necessary, Mr. Valmond."

"Sir, I am well aware of your feelings about me. But it is imperative that I speak with her. I'll come to the store if I have to."

"The store is closed. Out of business."

"Then I'll drive down and wait until you let her come out to talk to me. It's that important, sir. If I have to, I'll—"

"Paduah is dead! She passed away Saturday morning...."

Neither spoke for several minutes.

"What? How? She seemed perfectly healthy when I saw her last," Jean Claude said, unsure of Doc's willingness to go into detail.

But the details came in chronological order: her tearful return after the date, running past Doc when he asked what the problem was, closing her bedroom door, and the sound of her falling onto her bed. Doc woke up twice later that night. He could still hear her crying.

Coming down the stairs the next morning, he had conflicting emotions—anger at the source of his daughter's pain, and the joy of knowing it was finally over. He then went on to recount entering the storeroom and eventually finding Paduah's body.

Ending the call abruptly seemed the merciful thing to do. The press of a button stopped the bereaved father in mid-rant. Somewhere between "I curse the ground you walk on! I curse the first time you ever spoke to her!" and "The blood of my innocent little girl is on your hands!" Jean Claude managed a heartfelt "Sir, I'm so, so very sorry…." Probably never registered….

He rose, exhausted from the cherry walnut desk in his executive home office. Perhaps a call to Angeline would be in order. Last they spoke, she seemed to be in a good place after divorcing Albert a year ago. She'd thought about returning to France. Ironically, she didn't want to leave until he found true love. But he had no desire to discuss finding and losing that love in the same conversation with her.

Moving through the lavish French provincial dining room, he paused briefly at the Norwood entertainment center against the living room wall. A familiar cylinder sat perched on the top shelf.

"Alexa, play 'I Want To Know What Love Is' by Foreigner, please."

"'*I Want To Know What Love Is,' by Foreigner, on Amazon Music, starting now.*"

As the melodic tones of the intro filled the room in Bose surround sound, Jean Claude sank into his favorite recliner. He stared once again at the wrinkled copy of the *Kenner Star* on the oblong pewter coffee table. Images of Gigi filled his mind: her eyes, her smile, the softness of her skin, that childish innocence…her *smell*. Once again, tears began to fall.

He thought about consequences. Suffering, grief, humiliation, isolation—the price so many had paid for simply choosing to love him. And now Gigi—the one woman he could have truly loved—would never know how much she meant to him.

In the background, Dennis Elliot and the choir brought the chorus home:

"*I want to know what love is. I want you to show me….*"

Despondent eyes now drifted to the semiautomatic on the table—a promise in the dream….

He leaned forward. "Alexa, maximum volume here, please."

As the spiritual undertones began to fade—in one swift motion—in an act of self-inflicted, permanent relief—guilt, misery, pain and self-loathing ceased to exist. Jean Claude sat slumped, in a blood-soaked state of eternal rest, inches away from the headline that sealed his fate.

In the fiery depths of Dalhama, Goddess Fatima walked the aisle of crypts along the dark catacombs. She stopped to observe the latest inbound shipment. Her thorny fingers traced the fresh engraving: "*Apprentice Georgina Poncetrain.*"

"Did you not know, young fool, that I would be victorious despite your incompetence?"

And with gnashing teeth, she unleashed a monstrous shriek of laughter that sent earthquakes rippling through the dead zone. Demonic voices chanted their support in loyal celebration: "Nemo me impune lacessit! Nemo me impune lacessit!" (In translation: "No one offends me with impunity!"), an ancient Scottish motto favored by the Goddess herself.